Literally Twice

By

Ed Chandler

Contents

Second Chance

Hello, now as it happens I never actually planned to write a second book based around various things people say and that well if taken a little more literally then there might be a few problems and some possible humour to it all. It was after I'd realised that I'd lost something and then thought about losing other things that I then started this book.

What this second book does is show you a few more things that if you should say it, then do you really mean it and understand the true and literal meaning of the word and what you just said?

It's time once more to have a little fun and show that the English language is not as always straight forward as we'd like it to be...

Sit back and relax then as I get off to a good start as someone told me that they had lost their voice and yet somehow they still managed to talk to me...

Lost my voice

Have you really?

Have you ever read any of those newspaper ads about missing or lost items? Someone may have lost a bracelet, handbag, wallet or something and it has sentimental value, photographs in it that are the only existing photographs the person who lost it had...

Sometimes when you find something and hand it in and then the person who lost it actually get's it back, we're not there to see the smile or look of relief they get, but I bet it would make you smile...

Losing your voice then, well the thing is what we're really telling you is that our voice is not at its normal strength, for it's not gone completely, otherwise how else would you be able to say that "You've lost your voice" in the first place?

To lose it means that it's lost, gone not to be found anywhere and this would only be the case if you couldn't talk at all.

Now I yes in the last book I talked about "my voice keeps going" and you could argue this is similar, but this time we've said that we've actually "Lost" our voice, in that is has simply disappeared, vanished you could say without a trace, only it hasn't literally gone, for your voice is there, but it's just that you are unwell, or you have strained your voice, spoken to much, shouted too loudly and now your voice box needs time to recover before you can talk again.

If you smoke of course then you might later on in life
lose your voice because of cancer of the throat and
mouth perhaps, this is a risk of smoking naturally...

Saying we've lost something and in particular our
own voice would and will suggest that you lost it,
nobody else would have your voice now, would they?

After all a voice is a personnel thing, you can mimic
another voice, but an actual voice, the one you have
is yours and yours alone, so please be careful and
try not to lose it by over doing it...

After all accidents can happen and be careful in
smoky situations as well, because the next time
your voice is a little on the weak side, don't say
you've lost it, just say I apologise for my weak voice,
or better still just write it down...

Later in another Literal book there'll be a little part
about having a frog in my throat, then again this
could occur if one was eating frog's legs, but it
wouldn't be a full frog now, would it?

Lost my train of thought

Here's another one that begs more questions, for what is a "Train of thought"?

Do we mean a "Train"? As in an actual life size train, for that's a pretty big thing to lose.

Perhaps a train of thought is a small thing, like a model train, but looking in a dictionary I discover that the word "Train" first refers to this "To instruct in a skill" as well as "To learn the skills needed to do a particular job" and neither of these can be correct when applied to "Of thought"...

For although it might be possible to train your thoughts to specific things and a thought in particular, but if you lose this type of train as in to train the thought then you're still stuck at square one, right? After all we want the train of thought back, don't we?

What about to train for a sports event, or to aim a gun as in train the gun on the target or to cause an animal to perform or a plant to grow in a particular way, surely these also wouldn't make sense when applied to the thought part and so the literally thing to do is to clarify the particular train we have, if it's a diesel or steam locomotive, I mean...

If we clarify the word 'train' firstly then we can look at the next part as the words 'of thought' mean just that, the thing that it is "Of" it's not a train of dogs, food, people or anything else but 'thought' and as we know that the word 'lost' means as in not found, missing and perhaps gone, then we already know that in order to rectify this we could perhaps try and find what we've lost...

"Train" is also a line of railway coaches or wagons drawn by an engine and a series or sequence as well as a long line trailing back and section of a dress, it's even a line or group of vehicles or people following behind something or someone...

I guess the real literal sense of 'train' that we want is the one about a sequence or series, as thoughts can be like this, thinking of one thing and then another and then you want one more but you lose it...

Thought is of course the thing we lose as it's the past of think, as well as thinking it's self as in reflection and the concept of an idea.

Thought's are the ideas typical of a time and place...

So the train of thought we lose isn't a real train or any other type of train other than the one and only sequence and series that's more a sort of pattern. Something we are considering, but then lose our place in the series of thoughts we are having, our memory passes it by or something, perhaps the particular word is missing or something?

We say "My" as it's our own, for we can't lose anyone else's train of thought now, can we?

There's an interesting idea there, as sometimes we do lose track of a lengthy conversation and it's easy to lose many things in life, that's why the first part of this book is dedicated to things we lose...

If I lose my train of thought and not yours then it's
perfectly fine to say it was me who lost my train of
thought, otherwise, I'd say sorry but you've lost me
there on that or something…

Sometimes in this ever increasingly fast world where
multi-media devices and all manner of information
is all but a click away or so they say, well it's all
down to your own state of mind and how quick you
can process the thoughts going on in there and I
hope you've kept thinking and thought some more
about all this as it rambled on to a conclusion…

I may have started off with lost things for we all do
say these phrases and I've one more to do now, so
just hold on as we lose it and try to discover if we
actually had it in the first place…

Lost my marbles

If you actually own some marbles then ok...

If you don't and never have owned any marbles then I think you should never say this, for if you had "No Marbles" in the first place then how can you have lost them, because how can you lose something that you've never possessed?

What we really mean by 'marbles' other than the child's toy, is something to do with common sense, or mentality and the grasp of reality...

Sadly the only reference to 'marbles' in my dictionary is to the child's game of rolling marbles against one another. A marble is a small round glass ball used in the child's game marbles. 'Marble' itself is also firstly a kind of limestone with a mottled appearance which can be highly polished. Now I don't think you've lost this type of 'Marble' have you?

Also another use of the word "marble" proceeds the word cake as in 'Marble Cake', but the word is singular, 'Marble' and not plural 'Marbles' as to say you'd lost your marbles as in a reference to the cake or the type of rock would seem rather odd...

Recently as well I saw some adverts on television for a "Marbles" credit card, and you'd hardly want to lose this type of "marbles" as it might be very costly, in reality the original "Marbles" the glass Childs toy is the only true marbles that could be lost, so perhaps there'll be a sudden increase in people

purchasing 'marbles' just so that they can lose
them, but then why, what would be the point in
that?

We humans, what silly things we all are...

After all humans are as humans do or something
philosophical like that...

In conclusion to the whole question of losing things,
then so saying you've lost something would always
imply that this item was lost and that you at some
point prior to the lost had in your possession the
object or item in question. You have to have
something like marbles, a train of thought, a voice,
money, life or whatever it is, you must have or poses
it, in order to lose it...

Just a quick not here on the English language, I was
going to say "You need to 'poses' the item or object"
only I discovered the word 'poses' as in the noun for
the plural of a pose as in the sense of a position or
posture this word (Poses) is spelt the same as the
verb form 'Poses' as in to have something, to me I
thought the two would be spelt slightly different as
in order to establish a difference in a more literal
sense, you can see then the fun you can have when
you look up a word that has multiple meaning, but
also a word that has two different meanings, is spelt
the same but when it's a verb, a noun or an
adjective, then the word changes altogether
completely...

Well now that we've lost all that, I think it's high
time to get on with the book, not sure just what
'high time' is, but let's just skip it shall we...

Got myself in a big hole

Now how did you do that?

Were you just walking along, minding your own business and then suddenly the ground opened up and away beneath you and you ended up in a big hole? Or did you on purpose decide to start digging a big hole and then place yourself in it?

How big is this 'hole' anyway?

"Big" isn't very specific, for big to an ant could be something like an apple, but big to you might only be something like a room five meters square, big to someone else might imply the Empire State Building or something...

The thing is you've said that you've "Got yourself in" therefore you did it, you got into the hole as it were, so you must know how it happened, also you'd know how big the hole was, after all you're in it, right?

Maybe the hole is fictitious as what you mean is 'trouble' as in something you've said or something you've done something to upset someone and therefore the hole is metaphorical and not actually real...

I guess it won't matter, for they'll be a way out of the hole, all you have to do is find it, I'd lend you a ladder, but sadly I've not got one to hand, sorry...

Made from scratch

Anyone care for a slice of my lovely cake made from 'scratch'? Now why is it that no one as far as I know has ever asked just what exactly this 'scratch' is, is it some sort of magic ingredient that all good supermarkets sell, or perhaps it's from an animal, the 'scratch' of the South Pacific, first discovered by me. Well not really me...

I wonder if anyone is allergic to 'scratch' because then sadly anything made from it then they wouldn't be able to have any now, would they? You see what I've done is fallen into a non-literal trap and thought about just what 'scratch' is and where it comes from, because the more you think about what the actual reality of this is that the person who made for example the cake you now see before you did so from a combination of ingredients, none of which was 'scratch', but all of which, eggs, milk, flour and so on, the method and cooking was all done from these basic ingredients to produce such a lovely cake.

Scratch in a more literal and dictionary senses actually means as a verb to mark or cut the surface of a thing with something sharp, rub the skin with fingernails or claws because it itches, withdraw from a race or completion. Also as a noun it means a mark made by scratching and the action of scratching. It says nothing in my dictionary about a reference in 'doing' something, other than to withdraw from a race and that hardly seems logical if we've made this from scratch and the 'scratch' in question means withdrawing from a race, how does that even work or make sense?

Now I must admit that after the terms under the meanings of the word 'scratch' as a noun there's the following: - "Start from scratch = start from the beginning or with nothing prepared and "Up to scratch or up to the proper standard." There's no listing in this mini oxford school dictionary of mine, I'll just check another dictionary I've got, give me a second... (Laughter)

Ok in my Collins school dictionary I've got a fourth meaning listed as a verb saying "From scratch", just look in another dictionary, my Webster's one, I find the meaning 'To write awkwardly' and 'To strike out', 'A starting line for a race' (Not sure about that, but ok). Lastly then it was mentioned as an adjective and meant taken at random, haphazard, impromptu and also without a handicap. Sorry I also found it again as a noun meaning it's a sound made by scratching. Now I'm going to overlook some of these and stick to the first dictionary I picked up as this is the one I often refer to. I could however easily look the word up again and again, ask for a more in depth meaning and really over do it, when actually I just want to go back and scratch it all off, I think...

Do you know what I mean?

Well if anyone should know what I mean, it would be me, only if this book proves anything, it's that we'll all often and most likely say something and not really know what we actually and quite literally mean by what we've just said. I mean this whole rotten book has twisted words, looked at all their lovely and sordid meanings, discussed the very bottom of things, uncovered the truth, made things from this fantastic new material called "Scratch!" and to top it all I go and spoil it all by asking 'Do you know what I mean?'.

You see the thing is often someone will say this to you while explaining something that you most likely already fully understand and what they want to do is just check that you do know what they mean, that you understand it all. It's as if you don't comprehend them, but do at least understand them.

Mean in the more conventional terms of being nasty would hardly be suggested, but a literal possibility, none the less to suggest that I or you don't know what we mean and therefore ask someone if they know, well? It's a bit like asking a five year old, covered in pain, holding a paint brush, if they're the one responsible for the mess around in which they stand, with pain on the floor, walls and well them of course.

Stating the obvious should be another book I could write as we all do it, make a remark about something that is actually very clear, almost crystal.

Mean is also a mathematical reference, although I forget what for, but it has something to do with the middle or average number I think? I'm only basing this on my quick thesaurus search for the word 'Mean'.

The terminology of 'Do you know,' is very forward, it's direct, but the word 'what' now this conjures up a whole can of worms, for 'what' could just be about anything, almost everything it might seem, because 'what' doesn't necessarily have to be just one thing, or does it? 'What' is the subject, the direct object, the obscure reference perhaps and topic on which you're being asked a question, only if 'What' is say for instance the life history of the First World War, then there are more than a thousand references upon this subject, not to mention the previous events to and then during and afterwards.

All in all then it was some sadness that I do know and I both at the same time don't know what I mean, for I could mean many different things, it's all down to interpretation and life.

Found myself in a bit of a pickle

Here's one for all to enjoy, for it's a little bit like the big hole earlier, but this time the hole is more delicate than or not as bad as the prior situation for a hole even a metaphorical one would suggest something severe, a bit of a pickle might seem trivial compared to a hole...

Now the first thing to get right is the fact that you found yourself, because the term "Found myself" is just that, so how does one find oneself? This is a very deep question I know, but let's look at it in a more practical sense, as it's not a game of hide and seek with you playing by yourself now is it?

The term "Found myself" refers to you discovering this spot of bother or bit of a pickle, the problem at and that you now face, it's a simple problem to others but a little trickier to you, so some help and advice would be of great help...

Finding yourself can be done by looking in a mirror, for there you are looking at yourself right now, easy...

The more in-depth finding yourself might mean going on a long holiday or pilgrimage of some kind and would require a lot of thinking about...

What about this bit of pickle then?

Pickle is a sort of vegetable I think, I know you can eat them and they are often consumed by pregnant women so I'm told...

Pickle is also a sort of relish, a thick sauce for garnishing things like beef burgers. As pickle is a food really, so why use it to say that's where you've found yourself?

It's described as a 'bit' of pickle now just how much a bit is, well this is all done to literal and humorous interpretation, for a bit is not only a computer term, it can be referred to in as a "Bit on the side" a "Bit of cake" and all manner of things, so 'Bit' then the dictionary say's "1: A small piece of something, 2: the metal part of a horse's bridal, 3: the part of a toll that cut's or grips things when twisted."

"A bit" can be 1: a short distance or time as in "wait a bit" 2: Slightly as in "I'm a bit worried"

"Bit" is the past tense of bite, and it's also the smallest unit of information in a computer.

Now we've also said "A pickle" as in the food item, the more solid type of pickle, a long green thing to be eaten and not the type of pickle as in the famous type, actually the village of Branston is not far from Lincoln where I live...

So just what the bit, how you found yourself, and how much the bit is, what type of pickle and all that is going to have be considered when we look at this phrase some more, but sadly all we can do is find ourselves reading this book and in a bit of a pickle together, at least we're not in a big hole...

Back in the day

Which day? Often this expression is used more in the terms of "back in my day" a reference to day's gone by many years ago, for some they refer to the Second World War and the early to late fifties or even the sixties and up to about the year nineteen eighty.

The literal sense of the expression then is to convey the past, but which past and when might not be clear until the person saying the expression begins to recall their particular past life.

Back is the pre-tense expression of front and forward almost, as we refer to back as in previously and not a part of the body as in your back.

Back links to the word 'in' for without the word 'I' then we might be lost a little for what is it that the word 'in' does, well it tell us where to be exact, in rather than out, in as a preposition, in shows the position or condition as in at or inside. At is of course when and can be a particular moment. It's both in and at then, going to the reference point of the day, but the question will still remain as in to which day and when...

Day doesn't mean a particular day, for then we'd say Monday or Friday or another day of the week, so day can be any of the seven as well as any seven in any week in any month of any year, but mostly a previous day to the one you're currently on. Now the day might only be yesterday, but then the expression of "Back in the day" would hardly seem appropriate to say if we meant yesterday, I think then that there as to be a rule, a sort of unspoken rule as to govern a certain amount of time passing before you could happily and correctly say "Back in the day".

Just when or how long this is, I'm not sure, but I'd say it would have to be more than a couple of years, probably at least over five years, for we could easily say something like, "Do you remember a couple of years ago..."

Recollecting a moment in time is tricky as there any number of ways to get someone to recall a moment in time, you can say of course "Back in the day" and then go onto explain the period of time you are talking about, the particular year or even the exact day if you know it, after all some people can easily remember where they were and what they were doing on a particular day and time, especially if something important or trading happened...

Time then is not only very human for it controls us in many ways, governs what happens and influences decisions we make, but time is also a very particularly slippery and uncountable asset to us all, so please cherish time and look after it and I hope I've not wasted your time with this book...

The walls have ears

Well no they don't, unless you've taken actual human or other animal ears and placed them on the wall, so no the walls won't literally have ears will they...

However, if you say for instance have the dead stuffed head of an animal hung on your wall for decorative purposes, perhaps something shot by yourself, and just for clarity I'm neither for or against this as after all each to their own, which is another great saying but not one to discuss now...

Back to the ears on the wall then and the animal in question, most likely the head of a dear, then in this case we can say the walls has ears, but not 'Walls' unless more than one wall has a stuffed animal head on it...

I think then that this old saying came more from the Second World War when to talk about top secret things, or what or where your husband, loved one or other was fighting, go on training or something, well in other words, the enemy might well be listening to what you're saying, so be careful...

Also the reference to the walls having ears that in some cases walls aren't exactly sound proof and the noise of your conversation might well be overheard, there are some cases were thieves planning a robbery were caught so because they were heard in conversation discussing the event, so just take some care next time, for you never know who's listening...

Every hour God sends

First things first, in order for this to work I guess you have to not only believe and think that 'God' any 'God' is real, but also that in order for this 'God' to exist and for them to have control of time, well it's a lot to ask, is it not?

God is very questionable, for where did this 'God' come from, how long as this 'God' existed before we humans arrived and existed ourselves?

Time it seems has only existed since the very early days of man, for time before man is perhaps only being counted and recognised now, back when there was no man, was there time?

Looking at History closely, do we not see the birth of man, time and religion?

Thus then perhaps we have an explanation of 'God' in that in order for man to explain his own existence, he needed to do so in order to justify his own existence and so religion and "God or God's" came into being, created by man and a desire for knowledge.

Take a chocolate bar for example and giving it to a child, the child asks, "Where did it come from?", you say "Magic", as in it was created by you the all powerful being that you are, this is a very simple explanation, it takes very little effort to believe and understand, whereas, if we explain that a number of ingredients brought together, a company and a large amount of effort went into the evolution of the said

chocolate bar, then we have more and more
questions, but we can however trace most, if not all
aspects of the evolution of the chocolate bar...

To simply say that a powerful being, one not seen
and one not really known as to where and when it
existed and that this is responsible for the existence
having created it, well it seems to me that this is
where the questions should really be asked as to
why? When and how?

Why did or does God exist? What, when where and
how did or does God exist? And lastly why is this
God sending us an hour?

Getting back to it the literal part of this is about
'Every hour' as in each single hour we have and that
this so called 'God' is sending them to us, how we do
on to know and how some don't care or ask...

Only is God really sending us an hour by hour of
time?

Is it that no one really knows, not even if you lived a
model life of perfect health and happiness, then even
you and the best doctor in the world could not tell
you just how many hours you'd get...

An hour isn't that long really, but it's also odd that e
only get them one at a time, as the wording of "Every
hour" suggests this, it's not a plural as hour is
solitary and single, an hour, not hours...

It's "Every hour" and then skipping past 'God' as I've
sort of covered that asking who or what this 'God' is
and even asking where this 'God' is and the more

important question of 'How did this 'God' get all these hours? Why is 'God' sending us these hours and what for? To the last question of "How is this 'God' sending these hours?

Do the hours arrive one by one as if by magic? Does the postman deliver them to you each day?

Just how do you get sent an hour?

Is it not then literally impossible to send someone and hour? Or is the suggestion that I can give you an hour, not send you an hour, if I allow you an hour of time to do something perhaps, have I not then given you an hour, rather than sent you one?

Literal is as literal does then, or maybe not for this English, this odd language born many years ago, with Latin and Roman influence, Norman, Saxon, Germanic and French, Greek and Arabic even all thrown in together...

English today is not like English back in the day and as I lose some marbles, my train of thought and my voice! I discover the fork in the road, get myself into a nice big hole and find myself in that bit of a pickle again, but as 'God' sends me this hour to finish this book, sadly I recall that I don't believe in a 'God' or any type of one for that matter and when I die, if I've been told a lie and there is this 'God' then I shall be first in line with a very long list of questions for them or it...

Take care and all the best now...